Rhymes of Nature

Explore with Me at the Salish Sea

Rhymes of Nature

Explore with Me at the Salish Sea

Poetry by Nancy Oline Klimp

Illustrations by Jared Noury

Published by Nature Speaks To Us, LLC, Bainbridge Island, Washington.
Book design by Mi Ae Lipe (whatnowdesign.com).
Printed in the United States of America.

To contact the author or order additional copies:
NatureSpeaksToUs.com

First Edition, 2021
ISBN: 978-1-7351844-2-5
Library of Congress Control Number: 2020913679
Ebook ISBN-13: 978-1-7351844-3-2

MCP Books
2301 Lucien Way #415
Maitland, FL 32751
407.339.4217
www.millcitypress.net

To my grandchildren,
Adriana, Waylon, Easton, Otis, and Francis—
who teach me to "Notice nature's wonders."

The Salish Sea

A miniature ocean
Constantly in motion

Tides running forth and back
Sometimes active, sometimes slack

Runoff waters from the land
Mountain snows to shoreline sand

An estuary system ancient, large, and productive
Its diverse ecology, highly instructive

The Salish Sea is an inland sea that extends from southwestern British Columbia in Canada to northwest Washington State in the United States.

Its intricate waterways, inlets, and bays include the Puget Sound, the cities of Seattle and Vancouver, BC, and 419 islands, including the San Juan Islands near the Canadian border.

It is one of the world's most biologically diverse inland seas, home to 37 species of mammals, 253 species of fish, 172 species of birds, and thousands of types of invertebrates. Over a hundred of these species are threatened and endangered, and many people and organizations are working to conserve and protect them.

Its name comes from the first inhabitants of the region, the Coast Salish. Although these indigenous peoples are ethnically related, they come from many different tribes that each have their own distinct cultures, languages, and customs.

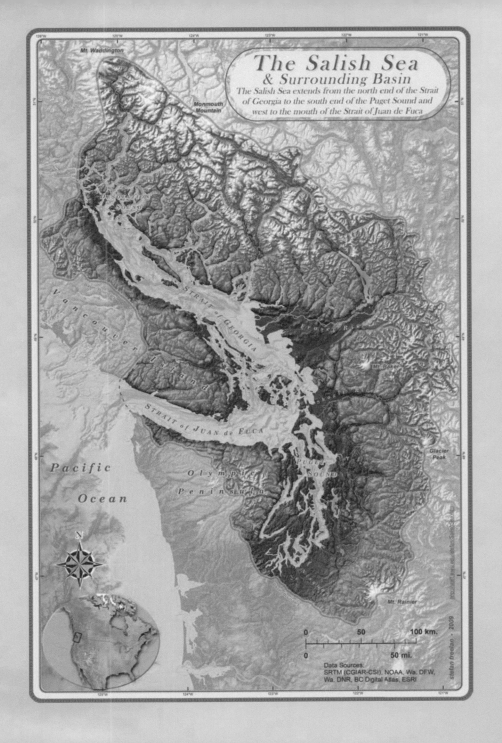

The Salish Sea
& Surrounding Basin
The Salish Sea extends from the north end of the Strait of Georgia to the south end of the Puget Sound and west to the mouth of the Strait of Juan de Fuca

Puget Sound

A fjord-like part of the Salish Sea
Underwater canyons form this estuary

Named for Peter, a sailor long ago
On his voyage of discovery, methodical and slow

Hundreds of meters down, a depth most deep
Where aquatic creatures swim, float, slither, and creep

This salty sea mingles with fresh water from the land
Back and forth in movement of rock, shell, and sand

Flooded glacial valleys carved out back in time
Follow nature's system of rhythm and rhyme

Mount Rainier

Mount Rainier, Mount Rainier
So huge, it seems so near

Rainier is guided from deep below
Its volcanic rumblings over eons slow

Tall and broad, planted well
A stratovolcano with a story to tell

Sometimes you see it—sometimes you don't
Above the clouds, its top seems to float

Native Americans called Rainier "the Mother of Waters"
The source of five major rivers—her aquatic sons and daughters

A super-high peak in the US of A
Where you can visit, climb, or hike one day

Glaciers

Snowfall froze, then warmth brought melt
These solid rivers traveled as an icy belt

Scouring, sculpting, slipping, and sliding
Over the land beneath, grinding and gliding

Ribbons of moving white
Traveling with gravity's might

Peaks slowly emerged
As the land converged

The Cordilleran ice sheet over eons so timely
Carved the environs of Puget Sound so finely

Canada Geese

Their group's called a flock, chevron, or string
At three months old, goslings take wing

They honk to communicate during aviation
Along their lengthy Pacific Flyway migration

In "drafting," a lift from the bird in front
Conserves energy via the flying V stunt

Under feathers, down keeps them warm
Protecting from all rain, cold, and storm

Bald Eagles

A shy raptor with vision keen and true
Named America's national bird in 1792

Representing strength and freedom
Flying up to ten thousand feet high—few supersede them

Gliding on rising thermal currents
Finding few obstacles or deterrents

With speeds up to seventy-five miles per hour
Seven thousand hollow feathers provide such power

They soar with spiraling swoops
In spectacular aerial loops

To capture prey, outstretched talons stand ready
Propelled by silent wings, strong and steady

The Sky

Gray skies cover
Raindrops hover

White puffy clouds billow
Appearing as soft as a pillow

Sun streams through, aims to warm
Then up comes a sudden, blustery storm

Skies unzip, revealing a quiet blue
Weather patterns change and renew

Boom!

Dark clouds gather, skies turn gray
The sun decides to hide away

Booming thunder is sometimes frightening
Then joined by several bolts of lightning

From above, a tumbling-down rain spray
Evaporates up to fall another day

Then it's over, passed, and gone
New weather arrives with a new dawn

Rainbow

When the sun meets raindrop
Look to the sky and stop!

Accompanying rain, mist, fog, and dew
A spectrum from red to violet and blue

Its colors are wavelengths of light
A meteorological phenomenon of sight

Light's reflection, refraction, and dispersion
Usher curiosity, wonder, and appreciation

A full circle it is but we see only half of it from land
Viewed from a plane, a complete circle rainbow is grand

Sun and moist droplets combine in a specific way
Adding a magical feeling of luck and hope to our day

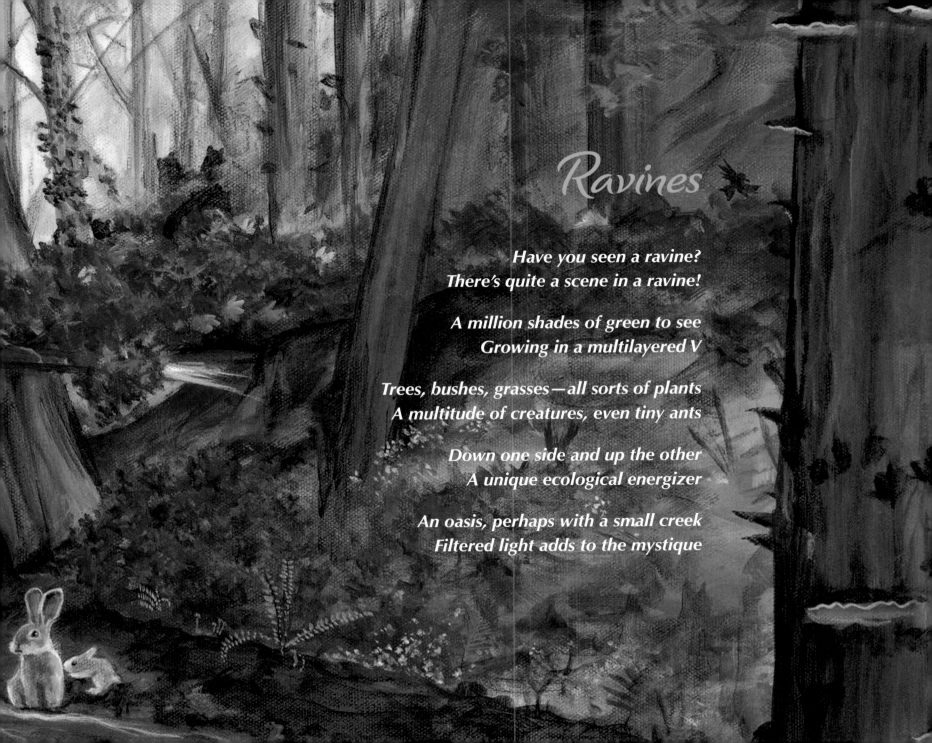

Ravines

Have you seen a ravine?
There's quite a scene in a ravine!

A million shades of green to see
Growing in a multilayered V

Trees, bushes, grasses—all sorts of plants
A multitude of creatures, even tiny ants

Down one side and up the other
A unique ecological energizer

An oasis, perhaps with a small creek
Filtered light adds to the mystique

Lichens

Lichens, from carbon dioxide to oxygen they convert
Their algae and fungus parts blend in a symbiosis concert

They gather water and produce food
Viewing them inspires a curious mood

When they're dry, "poikilohydry" is their dormant fate
When moist, photosynthesis and growth become their state

Find them on the surfaces of rock, soil, and tree
Three types—hair-like, leafy, and crusty resembling filigree

They grow from the tropics and deserts to polar regions
But their favorite environments are moist forest seasons

The Sky Circles
of Day and Night

They circle our Earth, around they go
Methodically pacing, not fast but slow

As circles of mass, they bring night and daylight
Cast your view up—they are often in sight

Obscured by rain, fog, or cloud cover
The moon and sun above us still do hover

Gravity pulls the tides to rise and fall
Affecting Puget Sound's unique features, one and all

Back-and-forth rhythms surge into harbors and beaches
Tides ebb and flow as nature moves and reaches

The cycles of circles around and around complete
Sun and moon guide nature to move and to meet

River Otters

You oughta see the otters
Swimming through local waters

Underwater acrobats, tails powering smooth sleek forms
Waterproof pelt layers keep them insulated and warm

They have long bodies and wide webbed feet
Some live in marshes where shorelines meet

Their gait on land is to walk, run, and bound
Semi-aquatic, they're everywhere all around the Sound

With a den for shelter and food everyday
They are free to play, play, play

Nocturnal, alert, and active mostly at night
They forage for foods to consume with delight

Green Darner Dragonflies

A hovering helicopter flying machine
Transparent wings of gossamer green

Flitting around ponds, marshes, and creeks
Washington State's official insect displays its techniques

Large with two pairs of wings, it seems very fragile
But they're skillful hunters—clever, strong, and agile

Darting in all directions, here and there
They've been studied for physics for which they've a flair

Butterflies

Butterflies, they flutter by
A quick hello, a swift goodbye

Flitting here, landing there
Going next to who knows where?

Sipping nectar from a flower favorite
In spring and summer, they'll savor it

With tapestry wings of patterns colorful
They fly in figure-eight motions powerful

Metamorphosis is complete in a matter of days
They develop and grow through each unique phase

To lobsters and crabs they're related
Butterflies are to be celebrated

Taima the Hawk

Augur hawk Taima flies through the tunnel
Leading our team as if through a funnel

His flight is a starting highlight
Fans begin surging with delight

The football game is about to begin
We hope the Seahawks win!

Taima's name means "thunder"
With crowds cheering, no wonder

Representing the team as their mascot
Taima is ready for the onslaught!

Let's Go Seahawks
Let's Go Seahawks
Let's Go Seahawks

Salmon

Born in streams and rivers, they head out to sea
To return many years later, their final place to be

From fresh water to ocean tides ever moving and slack
Osmoregulation offers adaptation for their journey out and back

Their names—king, chum, coho, silver, and chinook
They strive to avoid a fisherman's net, line, and hook

Their species are known as "keystone"
Central and vital to their ecosystem zone

Porpoises

What's the purpose of a porpoise?
A member of the cetacean's chorus

They almost disappeared but now they're back
And thriving—an important survival knack

Our world is visual, a porpoise's is acoustic
Echolocation sometimes sounds like music

They regularly stay near the surface to breathe
Uttering puffing sounds, similar to a sneeze

**As year-round residents of the Salish Sea
They're intelligent with playful personalities**

The Water Cycle

From the mountaintops to the deep, deep sea
Water forms and shifts constantly

Evaporate to precipitate, temperature is a guide
From gentle rain mistiness to heavy snows that slide

Back up it goes vertically skyward to ascend
As streams, rivers, and waterfalls all descend

Ice melts, brooks babble, rivers meander and flow
Clouds form, then down comes drizzle or flakes of snow

In circles, water moves around
Up to the sky and down to the ground

Tides

The tides come in, the tides go out
Waves unfurl everywhere and all about

The waves, the waves, they swirl and sway
Differently shifting from day to day

Currents tug this way and that
Water to shore, their moving habitat

"I know I've been here before—
I shall return many times more"

Guided by gravitational pulls and phases of the moon
Their rhythms keep in rhyme with nature's perfect tune

Ferries

Twenty-plus of them deliver back and forth their riders
Moving so gently, seemingly on gliders

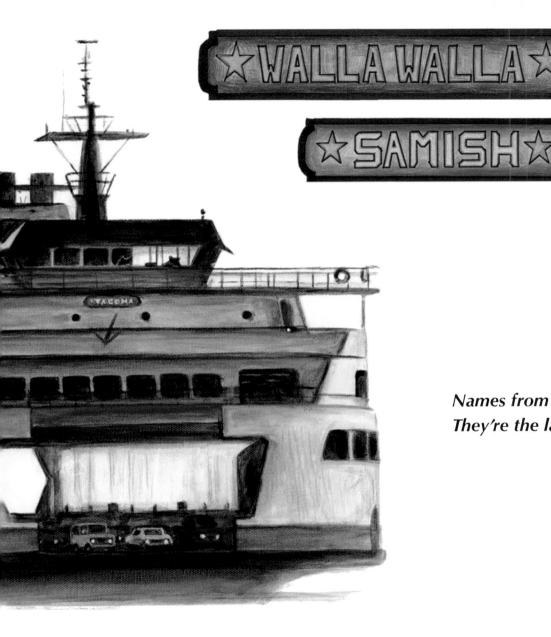

Names from many native tribes they derive
They're the largest fleet in America, continuing to thrive

Vessels

On Puget Sound a nautical collection gathers, varied indeed
These boats' captains who of the seascape learn and heed

They cast off and anchor, with journeys in between
Their marine knowledge fits into this blue-green scene

"Ahoy!" they yell in friendship or toot horns to alert their way
Staying on course, not to depart or stray

Freighters, trawlers, yachts, and boats go sailing
Barges and schooners in weather prevailing

They sway in waves, rolling in mist and spray
Under skies with rain or cloud covers of gray

Smooth gliding with gentle currents and sun
Makes their trips more easily done

Glossary

acoustic
Relating to sound or hearing

aerial
Performed in the air

algae
Simple plants that have no leaves or stems, growing in or near water

aquatic
Relating to living in or near water

aviation
The flying or operating of aircraft, helicopters, and other aerial machines

canyon
A deep valley with steep rock sides, often with a stream or river flowing through it

carbon dioxide
A colorless gas formed by the breakdown of plant matter absorbed from the air by plants

cetacean
A type of mammal that lives in the ocean (such as a whale, dolphin, or porpoise)

chevron
The shape of a V or an upside-down V; a pattern that geese sometimes fly in

cloud
A white or gray mass in the sky made of many very small drops of water

conserve/conservation
To protect or the protection of an environmentally or culturally important place or thing from destruction

Cordilleran Ice Sheet
A major ice sheet that covered parts of North America during glacial periods over the last several million years

dispersion
Movement in different directions across a wide area

diverse
Different in chemistry, form, and purpose

down
The soft first plumage of many young birds (such as ducks and geese)

drafting
Staying close behind another to benefit from reduced air pressure, thus conserving energy; geese often draft in a V formation

echolocation
The sonar system used by whales, dolphins, and bats to locate objects by reflected sound, for navigating, hunting, and avoiding obstacles

ecology
The study of living things and their environments

ecosystem
Everything that exists within a complex community of living things (such as plants and animals) and their environmental function as a unit

eon
A long period of time

estuary
An area where a river flows into the sea

filigree
A delicate ornamental design

fjord
A narrow inlet of the sea between steep slopes, typically formed by submerged glaciated valleys

flock
A group of birds or animals feeding, resting, and traveling together

forage
An animal behavior of searching for and finding food

fungus
Any of a group of organisms (such as mushrooms, yeasts, and molds) that produce spores, lack chlorophyll (the chemical that makes plants green), and feed on dead or decaying matter

gait
A particular way of walking

gosling
A young goose

gravity/gravitational
The force that pulls together all things; it keeps objects on the ground on Earth

indigenous
Living or occurring natively in a particular region

keystone
Something on which other things depend for support

lichen
A type of small plant that grows on trees, rocks, and walls

lightning
A bright electrical spark discharging within a thundercloud, between clouds, or between clouds to the ground

marsh
An area of soft, wet land that has many grasses and other plants

mascot
An animal, person, or object used as a symbol to represent a group (such as sports teams) and to bring good luck

metamorphosis
A major change in the physical form of something, especially some insects or animals as they become adults

meteorological
Pertaining to the science that deals with the atmosphere and weather

migration
The movement from one area to another at different times of the year

mystique
An aura of mystery surrounding something or someone

Native American
A member of any of the first groups of people living in North or South America

Look deep into nature and then you will understand everything better.

— Albert Einstein —

nautical
Relating to ships and sailing

nocturnal
Active at night

onslaught
A vigorous attack in a competition

osmoregulation
The regulation of osmotic pressure in an animal; salmon must osmoregulate to keep their body's ratio of water and salts properly balanced as they go from freshwater to saltwater and back again

Pacific Flyway
A major north-south flyway from Alaska to Patagonia used by migrating birds in the spring and fall

pelt
The skin of a dead animal with its hair, fur, or wool

phenomenon
A remarkable person, thing, or event

photosynthesis
The process by which a plant turns water and carbon dioxide into food when exposed to light

physics
The science that deals with matter and energy and the way they interact with each other

poikilohydry
The lack of an organism's ability to maintain the same water levels in its body when its environment is wet or dry

prey
An animal that is hunted and killed by another animal for food

There is no other door to knowledge than the door nature opens.
There is no truth except the truths we discover in nature.

— **Luther Burbank** —

Puget Sound
An inlet of the Pacific Ocean that is part of the Salish Sea on the northwest coast of the United States in Washington State

raptor
A bird (such as an eagle or hawk) that hunts and eats other animals

ravine
A small, deep narrow valley

reflection
Something bounced off an object or surface, such as heat or light

refraction
The bending of light rays or energy waves as they pass through one medium to another (such as the Earth's atmosphere or water)

river
A natural stream of water flowing in a particular course toward a lake, ocean, or other body of water

Salish Sea
An inland sea that extends from southwestern British Columbia in Canada to northwest Washington State in the United States

stratovolcano
A volcano built up from many alternate layers of lava and ash

string
A series of birds flying single-file one after another, often in a V shape

symbiosis
A close relationship between two different organisms that mutually benefits them

talons
The claw of an animal, especially of a bird of prey

tapestry
A heavy woven textile, often with complex patterns

thermal
Caused by heat or temperature

transparent
The property of allowing light to pass through so objects beyond can be distinctly seen

vertical
An upright position

vessel
A watercraft bigger than a rowboat (such as a ship, barge, ferry, or yacht)

visual
Relating to vision

volcanic
Relating to a volcano or made up of materials from a volcano

wavelength
The distance between the two peaks of a wave

Educational Notes

Salish Sea

See the Salish Sea section at the beginning of this book.

Salish Sea Marine Sanctuary | salishsea.org

Wikipedia | en.wikipedia.org/wiki/Salish_Sea

Puget Sound

The Puget Sound is an inlet of the Pacific Ocean and part of the Salish Sea in the coastal region of the Pacific Northwest in the American state of Washington, west of the Cascade mountain range and east of the Olympic Mountains. The term sometimes also refers to the Puget Sound region, which includes the Washington State cities of Seattle, Tacoma, Olympia, and Everett. Puget Sound is also the third-largest estuary in the United States.

The SeaDoc Society | seadocsociety.org

Encyclopedia of Puget Sound | eopugetsound.org

Mount Rainier

Rising 14,410 feet above sea level, Mount Rainier is the tallest peak in Washington State, visible from the city of Seattle and among the most iconic in the Pacific Northwest. Native Salish tribes called the peak Mount Tahoma. Still an active volcano, Mount Rainier also has the most glaciers of any mountain in the contiguous United States. It is renowned for its wildflowers and abundant wildlife, and many visitors are attracted to its year-round seasonal sports activities.

The National Park Service | nps.gov/mora

Glaciers

Glaciers are made of fallen snow that, over many years, compress into large thickened ice masses; they flow like very slow ice rivers. The Puget Sound topography is a result of powerful glaciers advancing and retreating during four different Ice Ages spanning hundreds of thousands of years.

Washington Department of Natural Resources | dnr.wa.gov/programs-and-services/geology/glaciers

National Snow and Ice Data Center | nsidc.org/cryosphere/glaciers

Canada Geese

Two groups of Canada geese live in the Puget Sound region: migratory and nonmigratory, meaning that some of them fly (migrate) to another place for the winter while others remain year-round. They are a large wild goose species that are often seen flying in a V-shaped formation.

Birdweb | birdweb.org

Seattle Audubon | seattleaudubon.org

Bald Eagles

The bald eagle is America's national bird. They are raptors, meaning birds of prey. They feed mostly near shore waters, eating live and dead fish; sometimes eagles capture a fish that is too large to lift in the air and must swim to shore with their catch. These magnificent birds were once endangered but are now thriving because of federal and state efforts to protect them.

Urban Raptor Conservatory | urbanraptorconservancy.org

Rainbow

A rainbow is a multicolored arc in the sky that appears when sunlight hits water droplets (such as rain), which act as tiny prisms. Rainbows contain seven colors: red, orange, yellow, green, blue, indigo, and violet. Rainbows are often considered a sign of peace and serenity.

Science Kids | sciencekids.co.nz/sciencefacts/weather/rainbows.html

United States Geological Survey | usgs.gov/special-topic/water-science-school/science/rainbows-water-and-light

Ravines

A ravine is a narrow landform with steep sides often formed by fast-moving water or glaciers eroding the land. In the Pacific Northwest, they are often hidden by lush forests or plant overgrowth; sometimes streams and creeks flow through them. They provide homes for many animals, mushrooms, and plants even in dense, crowded cities like Seattle.

Seattle Natural Alliance | seattlenaturealliance.org/2014/06/17/hidden-gem-orchard-street-ravine

Wikipedia | en.wikipedia.org/wiki/Ravine

Lichens

These slow-growing plants often appear as low, crusty, leaflike, or branching growths on rocks, walls, and trees. They come in many intriguing colors, sizes, and forms.

Burke Museum, University of Washington | biology.burke.washington.edu/herbarium/imagecollection.php

Salish Magazine | salishmagazine.org/lichens

Sky Circles

The lunar (moon) phase is the shape of the sunlit portion of the moon as viewed from Earth. Eight distinct lunar phases occur as the moon completes a full orbit around the Earth in just over 27 days. The moon is Earth's only satellite, and its gravitational pull causes the Earth's ocean tides.

National Aeronautics and Space Administration (NASA) | moon.nasa.gov

Future US | space.com

MoonConnection | moonconnection.com

River Otters

These playful, energetic animals are built for swimming with their long, streamlined bodies, short legs, webbed feet, and dense fur that keeps them warm. They can dive to a depth of 60 feet and hold their breath for 8 minutes underwater. They eat mainly fish but also frogs, crayfish, and crabs—some even use rocks to help them smash open shellfish!

IUCN/SSC The Otter Specialist Group | otterspecialistgroup.org/osg-newsite

National Geographic Society | kids.nationalgeographic.com/animals/mammals/river-otter

Green Darner Dragonflies

In 1997, students from Crestwood Elementary School in Kent, Washington, successfully suggested to lawmakers that the green darner dragonfly be Washington State's official state insect. As one of the largest, fastest flying dragonflies, it is an excellent aerial hunter. They are seen in the Pacific Northwest in early spring through the fall. Its family group is Odonata.

Learn About Nature, Dragonfly-Site | dragonfly-site.com

Burke Museum, University of Washington | burkemuseum.org/collections-and-research/biology/arachnology-and-entomology

In all things of nature there is something of the marvelous.

— Aristotle —

Butterflies

The butterfly has four wings, which are often brightly colored with unique patterns. They feed mainly on the nectar of flowers, and they serve as pollinators. Their life cycle has four parts: egg, larva, pupa, and adult. They use their antennae to smell and find food, navigate, and keep their balance. Lepidoptera is their family group.

Washington Butterfly Association | wabutterflyassoc.org

Project Noah | projectnoah.org/missions/30733144

Taima the Hawk

The game does not begin until the hawk flies! Taima is the live mascot for the NFL's Seahawks football team. At the start of every home game in Seattle since 2006, he inspires fans by flying through a tunnel that leads the team's players onto the field. Taima is an augur hawk that hatched in 2005 in St. Louis, Missouri. In the days leading up to a game, he practices his flights many times per day.

Audubon Society | audubon.org/news/what-seahawk-anyway

Seattle Seahawks | seahawks.com/mascots/taima

Salmon

A valuable food fish for both humans and animals, salmon are cultural icons of the Pacific Northwest. Living in the Salish Sea are the chinook, chum, coho, pink, and sockeye species. They are anadromous, meaning they can live in both fresh and salt water. Salmon begin their lives in creeks and streams, travel to the sea to spend their adulthood there, and return to their birthplace to spawn (reproduce), using their excellent sense of smell, ocean currents, river flow, and Earth's magnetic field.

Long Live the Kings | lltk.org

A Spot Tail Salmon Guide | salmonguide.com

Porpoises

Both the Dall's porpoise and the harbor porpoise live in the Salish Sea. Resembling small dolphins, they are sensitive, curious, intelligent animals. They are sometimes called "puffing pigs" because of their loud noises when they exhale near the surface of the water. They nearly disappeared because of noise pollution, loss of prey, and drowning in commercial fishing nets, but their numbers are growing again.

Encyclopedia of the Puget Sound | eopugetsound.org/terms/397

The Whale Trail | thewhaletrail.org/wt-species/harbor-porpoise

The Water Cycle

The Salish Sea region contains hundreds of microclimates, from the wettest place in the United States (the Hoh Rain Forest) to the warmer, dryer "banana belt" zones such as Sequim. Weather patterns are influenced by water bodies, jet streams, and mountains. As the sun's heat changes liquid water into water vapor, the vapor rises and cools, condensing into clouds. When the clouds get big enough, they release rain, and the process starts all over again.

United States Geological Survey | usgs.gov/special-topic/water-science-school/science/fundamentals-water-cycle

Tides

Tides are the rise and fall of the levels of the ocean. They are caused by gravitational forces from the moon, sun, and the rotation of the Earth. Two main types of tides—neap and spring—occur twice a month.

National Ocean Service, National Oceanic and Atmospheric Administration | tidesandcurrents.noaa.gov

Ducksters | ducksters.com/science/earth_science/ocean_tides.php

Ferries

Today's distinctive white and green ferryboats have grown from the original "mosquito fleet" of boats in the early 1900s that served Seattle and Puget Sound's many islands. Carrying nearly 25 million passengers annually, Washington State Ferries (WSF) is the largest ferry system in the United States and the fourth largest in the world. Each ferry can carry up to 200 vehicles and 2,500 passengers. Most ferry names come from Native American tribes and refer to a tribal group or local nature. Some examples are Sealth (Suquamish/Duwamish, for Chief Seattle), Tacoma (Southern Lushootseed: "snowy mountain"), Elwha (Chinook dialect: "elk"), Samish (Samish: "giving people"), and Cathlamet (Kathlamet: "stone").

Washington Department of Transportation | **wsdot.wa.gov/ferries/terminals/our-fleet**

Vessels

Puget Sound's deep-water ports attract vessels of all types and sizes year-round, supporting a huge maritime economy. Barges, ferries, container ships, auto carriers, bulk carriers, oil tankers, yachts, sailboats, fishing trawlers, pleasure boats, and tow and tugboats are just some of the different vessels you might see on the Salish Sea. They carry millions of tons of supplies, fuel, food, vehicles, and people every year. Fishing boats catch fish and shellfish in the Salish Sea or travel north from Seattle to the abundant waters of Alaska.

The Nature Conservancy | **arcgis.com/apps/MapJournal/index.html?appid=48918c38e9454f8794eb0c565c8a9e16**

Fisherman's Terminal | **portseattle.org/maritime/fishermen-terminal**

The Center for Wooden Boats | **cwb.org**

Acknowledgments

The author and illustrator wish to thank the following people and entities who granted permission to use their photography and map as references and artistic sources.

Harbor Seal	Mark Dodge (photographer)
Orcas	NOAA/SWFSC and Vancouver Aquarium's Coastal Ocean Research Institute, public domain
Salish Sea	*Map of the Salish Sea and Surrounding Basin,* Stefan Freelan (cartographer), Western Washington University, 2009
Glaciers	National Park Service, Loren Lane Photo, public domain
Canada Geese	Derivative of "Canada Goose, Burnaby Lake Regional Park (Piper Spit), Burnaby, British Columbia" by Alan D. Wilson (photographer), naturespicsonline.com, licensed under CC BY-SA 2.5

Bald Eagles	Jessica Romanyszyn (photographer)
River Otters	Nicole Duplaix (photographer)
Taima the Hawk	Rod Mar (photographer)
Salmon	Jonny Armstrong (photographer)
Ferries	Terry Birch (photographer)
Raccoon	Terry Birch (photographer)
Shimmering Puget Sound	Derivative of "Coast Salish Fish Trap" by Richard Eriksson (photographer), licensed under CC BY 2.0

I deeply appreciate the knowledgeable encouragement of Mi Ae Lipe, John Klimp, Florrie Munat, Hilda Weins, Alice Acheson, Karen Noury, Paul Heys, Tia Rich, John DesCamp, Karen Nelson, Pam Christensen, and Ben Schill. They have all proven invaluable on this "Meet Me Journey of Exploration."

Jared Noury's artistry has brought vibrant life to these poems.

Thank you, everyone!

—Nancy Oline Klimp